LETTERS TO THE

LENA BERTONE

thelitpub.com

Cover art and design by Jana Vukovic.
Prepress by sunnyoutside.

ISBN: 978-1-937662-10-3

Thank you, Molly Gaudry.

Thank you to Kriste Peoples, my dear friend and always my first reader; to Jennifer Pashley and Matt Tompkins for their invaluable help with this manuscript; and to Patricia Murphy, Jenn Scott, Susan Barnett, T. M. McNally, and my mom and dad for their persistent kindness and support.

Let me call you Sweetheart. I'm in love with you.
Let me hear you whisper that you love me too.

—Beth Slater Whitson

LETTERS TO THE DEVIL

THIS WAS MY LIFE
BEFORE YOU

I lived on a farm with my toothless invalid father and my sister. Our house was a shack and our farm was a yard of chickens and goats. We stole wheat and beans from the fields of the other farmers late at night, two in the morning, after everyone had gone to bed but before the first roosters crowed.

From the time I was seven or eight, my job was to make the bread and pasta, to bring the wheat to the miller, to do whatever he asked to persuade him to give us flour in trade.

CARISSIMO

This was my life before you

I lived with my toothless invalid father and my twin sister. Our house was a shack and our farm was a yard of chickens and goats. We stole wheat and beans and greens and fruit from other farmers at night, enough to feed us for a day or two at a time. I made bread and pasta. I brought the wheat to the miller, persuaded him to give us flour in trade.

I was eighteen when I left. My father was an old man. He had been an old man a long time. I didn't think of him as my father, but as the old man.

I had decided years before, when I was ten or twelve that I would not bathe the old man anymore. I would not dress him. I would not rub oil into his cracked skin or pick the rotting food from his gums. I would not talk to him except to tell him how much his existence disgusted and nauseated me. I would not wipe his nose or ears and I would not take him to shit or piss or give him my arm so that he could lift himself from the broken bench he sat on from morning till night. I would not smile at him because looking at the sagging skin of his face started a hammering rage in my gut, and I would not make the gnocchi he loved because he didn't deserve them. I did, however, soak his bread in goat's milk so that he would be able to chew it. I did this not out of kindness or compassion, but because I could not not do it. It was the least I could do.

I was eighteen when I left with my twin. We wore our best dresses. We held hands. We were looking for a prince. We found you.

I'm so lonely here without you

I'm so lonely here without you. No one will look at me. Your servants disgust me. They are like cooked poultry. Their necks are crooked, their heads cranked down to the floor like walking dead. I can't tell if their eyes have dried up or rolled back into their heads and they never look up and I don't know if they're unable or unwilling to look at me because of how I look or who I am, but honestly I don't care, or I didn't when you were here, but now, if they would just say a word to me, if they would just say Yes when I tell them to shut the door, or make dinner, or build a fire, or take the child. But they're silent, and old, even older than I am and feel, and every part of their faces is sunken in so that I don't know if they have eyes or if their eyes are dried up bulbs in those pinched, twisted faces. And what would they need eyes for anymore? There's nothing to see. They know this house. They've been here forever. Longer even than me and they mumble to each other but they won't say a word to me and they stop when I come near so that I can't hear their voices, what they say about me. I see their closeness, their collusion, and then they break apart and creep to their stations, chins down and gnarly hands curled into each other. It's so quiet except for the wind and their feet dragging and the boy's crying and my own voice and I want to hear them speak to me. I want them to ask me what I want for dinner, which bed sheets, what does the child want, Signorina? Take this child back, Signorina. If only they would say my name. I need someone to say my name.

But not them. I don't want them to say my name. I don't want to hear it coming from their fetid rotting mouths.

CARO

I'm so lonely here without you. I have the baby but he's no companion. He's no companion like you were. When will you be back? Where are you? I ask but I know you won't answer. I'm your servant and I'll do anything for you, but also I just miss you so terribly I don't know what to do. My arms and chest ache with sadness. My fingers ache with sadness. I'm getting old. My hair is half gray, but I curl in your chair and I ache for you. You are the same you you were twenty years ago

you will always be the same you Caro

but I am getting old and my fingers ache with sadness thinking about your soft hands, your palms on my face. I think about the sound you make

that growl that moan

when I push my face into your neck. I close my eyes and curl in your chair and live in that sound
in my ear pounding in my ear

I don't want to forget it. And then the boy cries and I have to put him in the closet or put myself in the closet because I can't bear to hear anything when I feel like this. You've been gone so long and it hasn't even been a year yet. I'm afraid to think how long it will be. How long do you mean to leave me here alone with this boy

I hate this child, this obligation, and I don't understand.
I know it doesn't matter if I understand—and it doesn't
matter if it makes any sense. When has anything you've
ever asked of me made any sense. You make no sense and
I love you, despite it being the stupidest thing I could pos-
sibly do. I am so tired tonight. I want to talk to you. He
wouldn't sleep and he cried when I tried to leave him and
his crying was so shrill and saw-like—the only thing I
could do to quiet him was let him sit on me and rock him
while I held him tight to my chest. When he whimpered,
I hummed to distract myself from the sound. I could
feel the boniness of my elbows and knees as my limbs
pressed together to hold him close. It was tiring, Caro.
This is shitty work. And as I was holding this soft clump
of body and tears, this thing sucking its thumb, I thought:
Why did I find it for you? How stupid of me. I didn't know,
couldn't have known, the consequences. I'm so good at
doing what you ask and you asked me to find the boy, like
a riddle. Find a boy in this house. So I found him for you.
In that corner. On that chaise. Under that newspaper. I
thought he was dead, he was so blue and stone hard. But

I brought him to you and your hand awakened him, and then you gave him back to me to care for. You gave him to me and he shit black tar shit on my gabardine trousers.

I think of your face. I sit in your chair in the library and think of your face, the first time you let me touch your face. My eyes closed, you let me sit on your lap, and your face, Caro, always a haze, always in shadow, you let me touch your face, and with my eyes closed, I imagined the skin of your cheeks was soft and fatty. Your cheekbones, set wide. Your beard, soft, smoky, red-brown. I touched your eyes and they were squeezed shut like mine. When I kissed you, your lips were hard and soft and flat and round all at the same time. I hooked my fingers around your ears and you breathed into my mouth. Your hand left a hot red print on the back of my neck.

I remember when—this was a long time ago. This was for about five minutes? I remember when you made me feel beautiful. or not ugly. or forget that I was burned and hairless on part of my head. or maybe you restored it because I remember your hands in my hair or maybe you made me look different when you wanted me to look different from how I look. Did you do that? I don't remember now. Maybe you did but it's one of those things I don't want to remember. How you made my breasts more plump and my hair softer and wavier. Chestnut, that color you like on girls and horses. Did you change my face? It bored you. It wasn't pretty enough. I never saw your face, love. I can't imagine wanting to change it, but maybe if I saw it? Could I tire of you? How could I tire of you?

Early, when I was still young, you dressed me up as a witch in a black Chanel suit and snakeskin pumps I couldn't walk in. I wore a hat and a beaded veil over my eyes, and you made me walk all over the city in those shoes. They dug into my heels and blisters formed at each of my toes but your voice in my head growled at me to go on, go on.

I had envelopes to deliver for you, and what was in them? I still don't know.

I don't know what those people saw when they looked at me, when they opened their doors. I don't know what the Farmacista saw when I stepped into his store. You had dressed me in that black Chanel suit and the lipstick I wore was a pale, sweet pink. The pearled veil covered my eyes but the Farmacista, when he saw me, stepped back and knocked a shelf of headache drops to the floor. He took the letter but he shook.

I don't know what the butcher saw when I pushed open his door and removed my white gloves. He gasped and crossed himself, shut his eyes and cried, a big man like that!, cried so that his chest heaved and I gave him his envelope.

I don't know what the old woman in her courtyard saw when I pulled open the rusty gate. My feet were bloody beneath my stockings, the blisters burst and your voice in my ear growling at me to go on, go on. Despite my bloody feet, my legs were shapely under the sheer black, a cramp like a fist in each calf. The old woman, when she saw me, she tried to run away to her door, clutched at her garden vines with her ugly tortured fingers, but old ladies are slow, and I grabbed her arm and pushed her down onto the iron bench. I made her open the envelope and read it, like you said I should, and then I asked her:

What do you see when you look at me? What do you see?

She wouldn't answer me, Caro. I grabbed her wrist, I nearly broke her dusty wrist, and I told her to tell me, at the very least, how much she liked my shapely suit.

MY LOVE

Remember the time you had me chase those tiny children in La Villa Bellini? They trampled our picnic but we had them for supper. It was so romantic. My sneakers were ruined but I have them saved to remind me. It was a lovely day, wasn't it?

They tasted so sweet, but I think

I think it was because of the way you looked at me.

MY LOVE

What did you see when you looked at me?

It's hard to think of the lovely days.

Most days were not lovely.

No days now are lovely.

X

I stood naked in the snow my clothes burned off my skin
burned off and I waited for your voice inside my head I
waited for I knew what you would say next, and then I
did what I knew you would tell me to do I did it before
you told me so that you would know that I knew your
heart so that you would know that I was the one who
knew your heart

I stood naked in the snow

This boy. This baby boy. You said he was yours or maybe you didn't. He was here, in the house, for the two of us to find. I'm taking care of him for you. Like you asked me to. Thank god you have other servants because I couldn't do this alone. They feed him, and clean him, and make sure that he falls asleep and wakes up, but I read to him, and I rock him, and I tell him stories about you.

Maybe I shouldn't talk to him about you. I don't know when you'll return. Maybe better if he thinks you're dead. Or if he doesn't know you existed ever at all. When are you coming back?

MY DEAR

Do you remember the time I wore a striped silk scarf and you carved an umbrella from an elephant carcass and it was big enough for the whole sidewalk?

Sometimes I behave as though you're his father and I'm his mother. I should stop that. Before he understands. You're not his father. You're not coming back. I'm not his mother. I'm his something. His caretaker. I'll take care of him. What else can I do? Someone has to care for him. I won't abandon him or leave him for dead. But I won't torture him with the promise of love. I'm not a demon like you. Well, I may be a demon, or worse, but I'll care for him until he can care for himself. Are you coming back? Am I asking you? I'm not asking you. Yes, I am asking you. In a letter I'll never send. In a letter I'm writing to myself, Caro. I miss you. I always always will.

CARO

I want to say bluntly. You broke my heart. So that it's clear that you did it and it still hurts and I think any moment you'll do it again. Every moment you're doing it again. You are not here and you're doing it again and I think every minute that you did it because you think I'm not good enough for you and you thought it and you think it and it's not true. And it is true. I'm not good enough. Or you think I'm not good enough. Or maybe I'm wrong. Maybe you're confused. Maybe you love me. Maybe you did. Maybe you will. Maybe it should be enough right now how it felt when you kissed me, when we kissed.

O our faces when we kissed.

DIAVOLO

I did everything you asked me to do.

I walked through fire for you. My skin burned off my face and fingers.

I walked through fire for you. I killed my sister for you. Pulled out her hot beating heart.

I walked through fire for you. Burned off my face for you. Killed my sister for you. Clawed into her chest with my skinless fingers and pulled out her heart for you. Before I even knew you I did these things for you. The idea of you, Diavolo. The presence of you in the sky in the lava challenging me wanting to overtake me.

Where are you now.

There is no presence. You're not in the air, you're not in the rocks. None of the endless rooms in this house, not in your library. You're gone from your library. And I watch this ugly thing grow—this vile biological fact—

this child—his hair, his face, his limbs, his fingernails and this is my only occupation while I wait for you to come back. This is what you left for me. I ache. I ache for everything. I ache for everything I don't have

I can't live in this house anymore.

Sometimes I find your notes, and I wonder if you left them for me. Cleaning out your ashtray, I found folded and burned: "Lacerate." Under your chair cushion: "Do not reupholster." Behind your supply of soap in the closet: "Lye-free only." Bookmarking LOLITA: "Is this love?" On the dried oregano in the kitchen, in your long, looped hand: "Use sparingly." Underneath the petticoats of the standing doll in my bedroom, a typed note: "Use caution when handling the fine and delicate materials herein. This is an object of the highest quality, suited for gods and monarchs, and its relinquishment to you is done grudgingly. Do your peasant best not to soil or otherwise destroy the exquisite work of art before you that you do not deserve to look upon, much less possess."

DEAREST

I'm trying white pillows on the blue sofa in the lounge. Don't worry! We can replace them when they get dirty if they're impossible to wash. I found these pillows and they have one great big button in the center. I think you would like them.

Tonight, when I put the boy to bed, I had that sweet idea again that I was his mother and you were his father and that together, we had made this dark-haired, dark-eyed baby, and that while I read to him, my somber face matching his somber face, you were waiting for me in your bedroom, or you had gone out to meet friends, or you were watching that stupid game show you like until I returned from the boy's room. I had this idea, and even as I was having it, I was careful to be gentle with it, to wrap it and tuck it and leave it as undisturbed an image in my head as I could. I was careful to try not to feel it. I read the boy his story, and then I read him another, and then without realizing, I fell asleep in the chair by his bed and had a half-sleep dream that continued my idea, in which you woke me from the chair and led me from the boy's room, and I could feel your fingers on my palm—your round fingertips—so smooth and hot, and you pulled me into the bathroom, you said, so that you could look into my eyes. There was an object, you said, stuck in my eye. You turned on so many lights, light after light, and you looked close into one eye (and

your face was hot like a light bulb) so that I could see
for the first time what your eye looked like—you held
mine open with two fingers and yours was glass blue, all
mirrors, all the way around, as though I was inside of it
looking out at myself looking back in at you and the heat
of all those light bulbs on my face, or maybe it was your
breath, always so hot, as you looked for the object in my
eye, pouring breath into my mouth, and my eye fixed
open, until my vision clouded and I woke up in the chair,
in the dark, the boy next to me, and you, Caro, not here,
not ever here, god knows where.

I don't want the boy. I'll send him somewhere. Do you
know my name? I'll keep him. I don't know. You never
said my name. I don't know how to raise children or why
you want me to raise this one. Is he yours? Is this busy-
work? You could have asked me to leave. Where are you

WHERE ARE YOU?

I think of you as "not here" but not much else. I don't want to think of who you're with because of course you're with someone so I just think "not here" like you disappeared between sheets of air, like you might appear from anywhere at any second, stepping from behind a flame, yourself a flame. But maybe you're in Greece, or Morocco, or you said you'd never been to Russia, so maybe you're there, in a house just like this one, below ground, and all the same rooms, all the same books in the library, the same servants making Russian food for you and your kitchen with a hearth instead of a stove and you with fur boots and a fur hat instead of crocodile shoes and a woman with you like me—with kinky gray hairs and part of her arm burned off, part of her neck red and shiny from the fire that joined her to you, and her hands like claws, and she calls you My Love. Is that what she's like?

Or maybe she's afraid to call you My Love, even though she loves you, because she knows you don't love her anymore, and she has some pride. Are you surprised that she has some pride? Or maybe she's afraid to call you My Love because it will make you leave her if you think that she depends on you for love or that she expects love from you or maybe she's waiting for you to love her again like you did once for a year or month or maybe it was five minutes or maybe? you're not so sure? maybe it wasn't even love you faithless beast? maybe it was just close?

Or maybe she's nothing like I am or was.

Do you remember the time you drove us to Taormina in the Fiat and we stopped at Naxos at midnight and it was still hot on the gray sand beach, and when we got back in the car you kissed my hand with your wide soft lips and we listened to the waves and watched Scorpio in the sky, and you asked me if I believed in God. I couldn't think of anything but you. I can never think of anything but you, and I said No but I believe in love, and you squeezed my hand and kissed my neck, the tip of your nose hot in my ear, and I thought . . . he thinks I mean romantic love, but that wasn't what I meant. Why would you have wanted that? Why would it have made you kiss me? I meant that other kind of love, that tenuous line, that invisible electricity that connects one person to the last and next, that delicate thing that's snapped and mended, snapped and mended. I didn't say anything. I didn't correct you, because you were kissing me and drawing me into your lap as if that tiny Fiat were melting into a raft and drawing us into the ocean. You were drawing me into your lap and I let you think what you wanted to think.

When I came here with my sister we were holding hands and I loved her more than anything. I loved her more than anything. I looked into her face and I saw my face, and it was young, and scared, and I held her hand tight, and laced my fingers in hers to say that I wouldn't let her go. We were wearing our best dresses with collars and belted waists and the elbows were worn from all the times we had worn them and the chests were tight because they were our best dresses and our only best dresses since we were fifteen. Hers was peach cotton with faded red flowers and mine all blue, worn out pale blue.

My Love, I was so young.

DIAVOLO

Come back

I lost you and you're still here. You are everywhere and yet I lost you and I can't have you and I never had you except maybe for five minutes, five imaginary minutes

I lost you in this house and I look for you in this house
in the rooms of this house I walk this house looking for
you I look in this night table drawer where I keep your
books the ones that remind me most of you the ones
that smell like you the ones you read to me when you
said for five minutes that you loved me but I can't look at
them and when I open this drawer to get my pens or my
paper or my shell flower necklace I touch those books
and they slide from my fingers they slide away from
me and I try not to see them while I keep them close as
close as I can keep them to me

I pretended we were married. You owned me. I waited weeks, months for one tender stroke and I feared that every drop of my existence dissatisfied you, disgusted you. This did not seem wrong to me. This is what marriage is like. You never turned me out. You never replaced me in this house and when you did touch me, when you did speak, you asked terrible acts of me. You trusted me. I was your partner. No other servant did your most gruesome work for you—the blood, and boiling, and skinning. You gave these gifts to me, and I accepted them. I'm trying to understand why I stayed.

You owned me. You gave me violence. I pretended we were married, because this is what marriage is like. I waited. I was willing to wait for your touch, which, Caro, is a sweet, soft touch, and your kiss. I can't describe it.

I waited a long time, Caro.

When he's old enough, I'll send him to school. And I'll be alone here. I'll send them all away, and be alone here. I'll close all the doors, and wear all my scarves, and light the fire, and sit.

THE DAY I CAME HERE WITH MY SISTER

Not the first day—the second day. I wore what I thought were my fancy shoes. I smoothed my curly hair with oil so that it bounced in long brown rings. My lips were full and cracked and red and I kept them shut against the vulgar space between my teeth. Sweet sister tells me to smile. The dog with the crow's voice leads us down a slender alley to your house. It's dark at noon and the rats chatter at us fearfully as we pass. My sweet sister holds my hand. In an hour, I will tear her heart out with that hand. She presses her chest to my back because she's afraid, but we both keep walking and fast because there are rats everywhere and I can feel your presence invading me from the inside. Already, I feel the pressure of you on my eardrums, your hands on my throat. Before you, I had no expectation that my life would be anything other than grain and anger and goat shit and injustice. With my sister pressed against me, I feel your hand on my heart, your forehead on my forehead, a premonition of something great. The potential for something great and beautiful. This was before I knew you.

Today I looked for the room with the blue bed. I couldn't find it. Did you make it blue for me that day? I don't think you would but maybe it faded or maybe it looked blue that day to me, that giant bed. I had to climb that bed, you lifted me onto that bed and the walls were dark with ageless soot because who knows how long this house has been here. Was it a Moor's house? A Greek's house? The Devil's house? I was still young and it was dark and you wrapped me in the sheet and pulled me atop your lap and it was dark and I couldn't see your face, but I could never see your face, not now, not in the light, not ever. You never let me see your face. But you let me kiss you, and we kissed as you held me naked with the sheet pulled tight around me and your lips on my lips as I touched your hair, your cheeks, your eyelashes, your earlobes. And how lovely this was, and I thought "lovely" this moment, I love this moment, I love you, Caro, in your lap with my legs around you, and you, kissing me so sweetly with your soft lips, your tongue, and I wanted to say "I love you," and it would have been so easy and so true, my heart full of you, but this was after—this moment was after you stopped loving me, so I stopped myself from saying it, this lovely thing I felt that I wanted to say this thing that was aching its way from my heart to my lips. Instead I said your name: I whispered it to your mouth over and over again hoping you would understand my heart, but you asked me, are you coming? are you going to come? And I said nothing. But I held you, stupid man, as long as I could.

On the first day I traveled here with my sister.

Do you remember the first day? Who were we to you?

We were searching for a prince.

We had only each other.

We were lost in a strange place.

We looked for signs.

We entered the dark and we were fascinated.

We didn't want to be peasants anymore.

We would do anything.

The crow with the dog's voice led us away from the castle. All the girls stood in line, but the crow called us with those words that weren't words, and of course we knew what it wanted, and what it wanted was what we wanted, so we came. We left behind the girls in line, almost every one with better shoes and better dresses than what we had—not that it would have mattered— what do little things like shoes and dresses mean when you're a queen searching for just the right little woman to be your son's wife? I wore blue, my sister wore peach, and we walked through the city and followed the signs you left for us, our brains electric with the possibilities of the day, maybe our lives.

The crow with the dog's voice perched at the top of a long flight of stairs down into the earth, and then as it started to flap and dive, we followed, and when your ancient, ornate doors opened, my sister restrained me from running inside. Running to you, whoever you were, was what I wanted to do.

And when we came in, we heard your voice. You told us to leave and never come back.

You didn't show yourself to us. Not the first day. But you wanted us. You chose us. You chose me.

DEAREST

I was such a fool for you, and for so long.

There is some happiness in being a fool. But then, when it's over, you realize how foolish it was to have been happy. This child smiles. At me. As though, through some fluke or error, it believes it can perpetrate a bond with me. I do feel sorry for it. The servants seem no better able to provide human nurturing than I am, though as far as I know, we are all human.

Maybe I can find the boy a home, or a school, or an orphanage, and he can grow to be a normal adult who remembers little or nothing about me or this house. Because I know you're not coming back. I'm not going to count on some flimsy promise that you'll come back once I've raised him. Because you're not coming back. Surely, you're not coming back to me. You're not coming back. I know this.

Most days, I know this.

There was the time I'd returned from Egypt. You'd had me scare someone or eviscerate something, or eviscerate some small something to scare someone and I felt so beautiful—my waist so small in a Valentino dress belted with a pink bow. My head was covered with a wide flowy hat that I wore pinned to my hair and my arms were covered in long pale gloves. I felt the salty breeze through both. I tasted it with my teeth. I was returning to you. I'd taken the shoes of the woman I'd blinded— that's it—that's what I'd done. Her shoes were jeweled, gilded, majestic—so incredible I couldn't leave them behind. The heel, so tall, was stacked with purple crystals and the edges sparkled so brightly in the sun I imagined I was walking in diamonds. Look down at these shoes and there was one huge stone on each, yellow and bright, looking back at you, and a peeptoe, of course. Happiness. Who would give a woman such shoes?

They were exactly my size. I put them on and glided out of that jeweled house, away from that beautiful screaming woman, back to you. I can never think of anything but you. I walked with purpose from that house to the dock, to the boat, to the ocean that separated us, eager and desperate to cross, my pink bow just ahead of me. What will you think of these shoes? I thought. How much will you love these shoes?

I don't know where the shoes are now. Are they in one of these rooms?

They were exactly my size. I put them on and glided.

NOTES

Because this story is written to represent handwritten letters / journal entries, I have foregone the use of italics, though many pages contain foreign words that readers might expect to be italicized. I have also chosen to eliminate end punctuation in many cases, and have broken lines and paragraphs in varying, but deliberate, ways.

The narrator of this piece originated in a chapter of my unpublished novel *La Revengista,* in which her story was told in a superficial and tangential way, as part of a gruesome fairy tale. I felt disturbed and haunted by her broken relationship with her sister, and by her passion for the devil, and wrote about it in this piece in the form of letters she might have written with the intent to send. But she doesn't know where the devil is, or when he'll return, so the letters become like a journal for her: both a place where she can write to him and a place where she can return to express her broken heart.

LENA BERTONE lives, writes, and teaches in Central New York. She completed an MFA in Fiction from Arizona State University in 2006. A chapbook collection of her short fiction, *Behind This Mirror*, is available from Origami Zoo Press.

www.ingramcontent.com/pod-product-compliance
Lightning Source LLC
Chambersburg PA
CBHW070506170726
48291CB00008B/2679